POKéMON ™

CATCH OSHAWOTT!

A POKÉMON LOOK & LISTEN SET

BOOK · DVD · HEADPHONES

Watch three episodes of *Pokémon: Black & White*, starring Oshawott,
using the collectible Oshawott headphones! Read about Oshawott in the 32-page book!

Catch Oshawott! A Pokémon Look & Listen Set

Your Look & Listen Set comes with a DVD of three action-packed TV episodes and specially designed headphones, all customized to your Look & Listen Set Pokémon!

Publisher: Heather Dalgleish
Writer: Lawrence Neves
Designers: Tyler Freidenrich and Megan Sugiyama
Art Director: Eric Medalle
Product Development: Drew Barr
Headphone Sculpting: Martin Meunier
Production Management: Jennifer Marx
Production Assistance: Katie del Rosario and Michael del Rosario
Product Approval Manager: Phaedra Long
Product Approval Associate: Katherine Fang
Editors: Michael G. Ryan & Eoin Sanders (for Pokémon) and Ben Grossblatt (for becker&mayer!)

The Pokémon Company INTERNATIONAL

Published by
The Pokémon Company International
333 108th Avenue NE, Suite 1900
Bellevue, Washington 98004 U.S.A.

1st Floor Block 5, Thames Wharf Studios, Rainville Road
London W6 9HA United Kingdom

11 12 13 14 15 9 8 7 6 5 4 3 2 1

Produced by becker&mayer!
11120 NE 33rd Place, Suite 101
Bellevue, Washington 98004 U.S.A.
www.beckermayer.com

becker&mayer!
BOOK PRODUCERS

ISBN: 978-1-60438-158-0

11542

Printed in Hangzhou China, 11/11

Visit us on the Web at www.pokemon.com

Welcome to the world of Pokémon! In this book, you'll learn about their world and the new region of Unova, home to many different Pokémon!

OSHAWOTT

SNIVY

TEPIG

WHAT ARE POKÉMON?

Pokémon are amazing creatures that can be found throughout the different areas in the Pokémon realm! High grasses, swampy marshes, and mysterious forests are all teeming with wild Pokémon, but you can also find them in bustling cities and busy towns. Each species of Pokémon has its own special traits and powers.

Some Pokémon evolve, or grow, into other Pokémon. For instance, Oshawott may grow up through training and experience into Dewott, and then later into Samurott. In Unova, Ash sees so many new Pokémon, it makes his head spin!

WHAT ARE POKÉMON TRAINERS?

In the Pokémon world, humans live, work, and play alongside Pokémon. Pokémon Trainers are people who want to make a life's work out of training, befriending, and competing with their Pokémon in Pokémon battles. Great Trainers try their hardest to understand and communicate with their Pokémon through love and friendship.

MEET ASH!

ASH KETCHUM

Ash Ketchum is on a quest to become a Pokémon Master. His journey has taken him to some incredible places and has included lots of adventures! Now in Unova with his trusty Pikachu by his side, Ash moves forward in his mission to be the best Trainer around!

Pikachu, an Electric-type Pokémon, has been with Ash since the beginning, but does not like to travel in a Poké Ball. Instead, it travels side-by-side with Ash, forming a true partnership like no other in the world of Pokémon!

The object Ash is holding is a Poké Ball, one of the special tools of Pokémon Trainers. There's more to learn about them. Turn the page to see!

POKÉDEX

The Pokédex is like a digital encyclopedia for Pokémon Trainers. Its vast collection of information makes it one of the most useful tools in a Pokémon Trainer's arsenal.

The Pokédex is also used to record and analyze data on never-before-seen Pokémon, so it's perfect for a region like Unova, where Ash is a newcomer and unfamiliar with the Pokémon living there.

The Pokédex contains a wealth of data about known Pokémon. But a Trainer usually has to see the Pokémon first so that the Pokédex can record the data. Then, the Trainer can use the Pokédex to learn more about it.

XTRANSCEIVER

The Xtransceiver is a new gadget unique to the Unova region. It allows Trainers to call one another and set up battles, and it uses a live video feed so that Trainers can see who's calling.

Pokémon Trainers know that Xtransceiver is pronounced *cross transceiver*.

POKÉ BALLS

Poké Balls are absolutely essential gear for Pokémon Trainers who want to capture and train Pokémon. The Poké Ball is an electronic storage chamber for Pokémon. When Ash wants a Pokémon, he throws a Poké Ball. When it opens, it captures the Pokémon and stores it until released. This is how Ash caught Oshawott, Snivy, *and* Tepig!

There are many types of Poké Balls, and each has a unique purpose and strength. Here are some of them!

A Pokémon Trainer will usually receive several of these right at the start of their adventure, along with a Pokédex! These standard Poké Balls are good for the Pokémon you first meet, but serious Trainers will know all about the other Poké Balls they might come across.

DIVE BALL
Works especially well on Pokémon that live underwater.

MASTER BALL
The best Poké Ball, with the ultimate level of performance. It will catch any wild Pokémon without fail.

NET BALL
Effective in catching Bug- and Water-type Pokémon.

GREAT BALL
Has a higher rate of success in catching Pokémon than the standard Poké Ball.

DUSK BALL
Works much better at night or in gloomy places, like caves.

HEAL BALL
Completely heals the wild Pokémon that it catches, which is great when a Trainer has worn down a Pokémon during an encounter.

ULTRA BALL
Has even higher rates of success than the Great Ball.

LUXURY BALL
Causes Pokémon caught in it to become more attached to their owners.

REPEAT BALL
Effective for capturing Pokémon that have previously been caught once.

Now that you know about Pokémon and the Trainers who battle with them, it's time to follow Ash and explore Unova!

WELCOME TO THE UNOVA REGION!

Ash has started his journey across Unova. He's excited about discovering new Pokémon. He's also got a whole new region to explore and many important people to meet!

The Unova region is filled with colorful cityscapes, lush forests, and forbidding mountain ranges. The people there are just as fascinating as the Pokémon. Pokémon Battle Club managers, rambunctious and exotic Trainers, and even kind-hearted Gym Leaders abound in Unova.

ROUGH WEATHER

Soon after arriving in Unova, Ash and Pikachu witness a strange event. A huge, mysterious thundercloud shooting out weird blue lightning hovers in the sky. Pikachu is zapped and experiences strange effects. Could the cloud have something to do with the legend of Zekrom?

PROFESSOR JUNIPER

The authoritative professor of the Unova region, Professor Juniper is a friend of Professor Oak's and a legitimate force in the world of Pokémon. She researches Unova and its unique Pokémon. Professor Juniper is the one who discovers what's gone wrong with Pikachu's Electric-type attacks.

"Zekrom is a legend in these parts. From within its thundercloud, Zekrom watches over people and Pokémon."

NEW FRIENDS

Ash befriends two new Trainers and their Pokémon on his journey through Unova!

IRIS

Iris is one of the first people to befriend Ash in the Unova region. She's an active nature-lover who is skilled at gathering fruit from treetops! But don't let her athletic ways fool you. She's all heart and is completely devoted to her Pokémon, Axew.

When Iris first meets Ash, it is under the worst circumstances—Team Rocket is trying to steal her Axew! Ash saves Pidove, Pikachu, and Axew, and Iris realizes that although Ash acts like a kid sometimes, he is completely dedicated to his Pokémon and to all Pokémon in general!

Although Iris is training her Axew, so far it has done little battling. It can use its powerful Dragon Rage move but not with a lot of control.

AXEW

TYPE: Dragon
CATEGORY: Tusk Pokémon
HEIGHT: 2'00"
WEIGHT: 39.7 lbs.

Axew uses its tusks to crush berries for food and cut gashes in trees to mark its territory. Its fangs become strong and sharp as they constantly grow back; even if one breaks, a replacement grows in quickly.

CILAN

Along with his two brothers, Cilan is a Gym Leader at the Striaton City Gym. He's a stylish, intelligent opponent whose strength is sizing up the relationship between a Pokémon Trainer and that Trainer's Pokémon.

Cilan is a Pokémon Connoisseur, a title that Ash has never heard of before. After Ash defeats him and wins the Trio Badge, Cilan sees the potential in Ash and asks to join his crew!

Cilan's trusty Pansage is just as good natured as its owner, but it's no pushover. It is a capable and experienced battler.

PANSAGE

TYPE: Grass
CATEGORY: Grass Monkey Pokémon

HEIGHT: 2'00"
WEIGHT: 23.1 lbs.

Pansage lives in the depths of the forest. The edible leaf on its head has stress-relieving properties, and Pansage shares this leaf with tired-looking Pokémon.

ALLIES...

BIANCA

Ash and Iris meet Bianca and her Pokémon, Pignite, on their way to Nacrene City. Bianca was sent by Professor Juniper with a badge case for Ash, but it is stolen by a Minccino. Don't worry—Ash got it back!

MINCCINO

NURSE JOY

Nurse Joy is the name for the entire league of healing women who staff Pokémon Centers throughout the Pokémon world. Pokémon receive the care they need to heal in these Centers. The Nurse Joy in Unova has 16 sisters who are also Nurse Joys in the region.

Nurse Joys usually have helping Pokémon as their assistants. In Unova, it's Audino, which uses sound to diagnose Pokémon.

AUDINO

AND RIVALS!

TRIP

Trip is the first competitor Ash meets in Unova. A very aggressive Trainer, Trip thinks Ash is from the "boonies" and assumes Ash doesn't know anything about Pokémon battling. Ash doesn't get the upper hand the first couple of times they battle. He loses his first battle to Trip because of temporary problems with Pikachu's Electric-type attacks, and then he loses a key five-on-five battle at the Pokémon Battle Club in Luxuria Town. But Trip will get what's coming to him...and soon. Ash is never one to take a defeat lying down!

JESSIE, JAMES, AND MEOWTH

These Team Rocket schemers never stop trying to thwart Ash and his crew, but they usually end up falling far short of their goal of world domination. Still, they persistently go through with some of the most outrageous plans imaginable—all while trying to impress their boss. Although other Team Rocket agents exist, these are the ones who have been a constant thorn in Ash's side.

THE ADVENTURE BEGINS...

...with these three Pokémon!

At Professor Juniper's lab in Nuvema Town, Ash gets to see the three starter Pokémon of the Unova region. In Unova, new Trainers choose their first Pokémon—Oshawott, Snivy, or Tepig!

OSHAWOTT

HEIGHT: 1'08"
WEIGHT: 13.0 lbs.

A Water-type Pokémon, Oshawott is great when battling Fire-type Pokémon. Oshawott is the one to choose for Trainers who like their battles wet and wild!

SNIVY

HEIGHT: 2'00"
WEIGHT: 17.9 lbs.

A Grass-type Pokémon, Snivy is quick and intelligent. Snivy learns fast and is an awesome choice against Water-type Pokémon.

TEPIG

HEIGHT: 1'08"
WEIGHT: 21.8 lbs.

A Fire-type Pokémon, Tepig can heat things up in a hurry. Tepig is dangerous against Grass types and will battle for you valiantly.

To learn more about Pokémon types, turn the page.

POKÉMON TYPES

Pokémon are classified by their type. Some are Grass types, which means they are susceptible to Fire-type attacks, while others are Fire types, which means that Water-type moves would be very effective against them. Water types want to watch out for Electric-type attacks and Grass-type attacks.

WATER TYPE VS. ELECTRIC TYPE

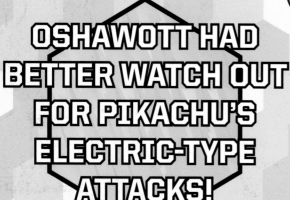

OSHAWOTT HAD BETTER WATCH OUT FOR PIKACHU'S ELECTRIC-TYPE ATTACKS!

THE 17 TYPES

BUG

GRASS

DARK

GROUND

DRAGON

ICE

ELECTRIC

NORMAL

FIGHTING

POISON

FIRE

PSYCHIC

FLYING

ROCK

GHOST

STEEL

WATER

Dual-type Pokémon

Some Pokémon can even be two types at once, like Woobat, which is a Psychic- and Flying-type Pokémon. And when some Pokémon evolve, their Evolutions change types. It's like when Tepig (a Fire type) evolves into Pignite (a Fire- and Fighting-type).

WOOBAT

OSHAWOTT AT A GLANCE

Now it's time to meet a special Oshawott that befriends Ash on his Unova adventure!

Could these freckles have possibly been short whiskers long ago?

Oshawott has five bubbles on its collar.

Its scalchop is made from the same material as claws, rendering it a dangerous weapon in battle.

Oshawott walks on two feet on land but uses its tail when it swims in the water.

WHAT IS...

a scalchop?

A scalchop is a razor-like shell that Oshawott displays on its belly. Oshawott can detach the scalchop and use it as a weapon, as seen when it popped Team Rocket's balloon while trying to save Pikachu and Axew!

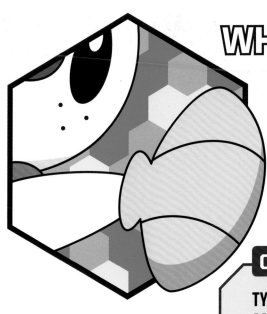

OSHAWOTT

TYPE: Water
CATEGORY: Sea Otter Pokémon

Oshawott attacks and defends using the scalchop that can be removed from its stomach.

Oshawott is a Water-type Pokémon that befriends Ash right from the start! It's shy and mischievous, but it's definitely helpful!

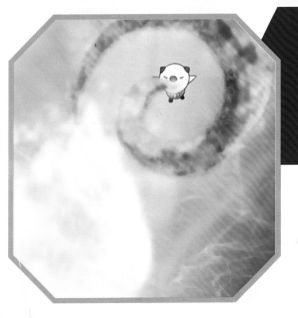

Oshawott is a formidable opponent in battle as well. Perfecting its use of the Water Gun move, Oshawott learns to turn the tables on quite a few Pokémon. Although Iris wants Oshawott for her very own, Oshawott takes a shine to Ash and agrees to join our friends on their quest through Unova.

Oshawott battles with both a traditional and a non-traditional Pokémon arsenal. It can use and learn moves like Aqua Jet and Water Gun, but it can use its scalchop for defense as well!

KEY MOVES

Here are some crucial moves that Ash's Oshawott knows. When Oshawott battles using these moves, watch out!

Tackle

Tackle, although a basic move, still manages to help Oshawott out in tight situations. It's a strong, head-on move that Oshawott is not afraid of using!

Water Gun

Water Gun is another basic move that is effective in a simple type-on-type matchup, like against a Fire-type Pokémon. Oshawott uses its Water Gun move extensively, but Water Gun could prove to be weak against tougher opponents.

Razor Shell

Oshawott's Razor Shell move uses its scalchop to slice and dice. It can cut down a target's defenses or deflect a competitor's blows. If Oshawott loses its scalchop, it will be in trouble.

Aqua Jet

When Ash trains Oshawott in the Pokémon Battle Club, it finally learns the Aqua Jet move. Oshawott's aim is slightly off, but when it does get control of Aqua Jet, it will be one of the most powerful Water-type moves it knows.

YOU SAY YOU WANT AN EVOLUTION?

Well, all right! Take a look at Oshawott's potential Evolutions!

Oshawott begins as a cute and cuddly marshmallow. But it is one sweet character that is ready to do battle at a moment's notice. Of course, Ash's Oshawott can react a little too impulsively at times!

DEWOTT

TYPE: Water
CATEGORY: Discipline Pokémon
HEIGHT: 2'07"
WEIGHT: 54.0 lbs.

Each Dewott has its own double-scalchop technique. Dewott know their scalchops must be kept in good condition.

Dewott isn't so cute, and it's far less cuddly—especially with the new-and-improved scalchops that it wields. It's large and in charge, and super-fast, too!

OSHAWOTT'S EVOLUTION

SAMUROTT

TYPE: Water
CATEGORY: Formidable Pokémon
HEIGHT: 4'11"
WEIGHT: 208.6 lbs.

Instead of a scalchop, each Samurott wields a massive sword formed from the armor on its front legs.

Samurott looks far more serious than Oshawott does—which just proves that you can't judge a Pokémon by its beginning form! Although we haven't seen much of Samurott yet, rest assured it is no marshmallow!

ASH MEETS OSHAWOTT

On his way to Striaton City with Iris in tow, Ash is befriended by Oshawott, and their journey as Trainer and Pokémon begins. But the journey takes a detour when they meet Dan.

When Ash and Iris are on their way to the Striaton City Gym, they fall into a giant hole. Dan, a local boy whose family runs the nearby hot springs hotel and spa, rescues them.

Wild Sandile are acting strangely, and Ash and Iris discover the cause: the Sandile are trying to protect nearby Deerling, Patrat, and even humans from a series of geysers threatening the safety of the hotel and spa!

The Oshawott from Professor Juniper's lab has been following Ash and wants to join him!

A sunglasses-wearing Sandile kidnaps Oshawott and Pikachu in an attempt to get them away from the spa!

SANDILE

TYPE: Ground-Dark
CATEGORY: Desert Croc Pokémon
HEIGHT: 2'04"
WEIGHT: 33.5 lbs.

A dark membrane protects Sandile's eyes from the sun. Sandile burrows in the sand with its eyes and nose sticking out.

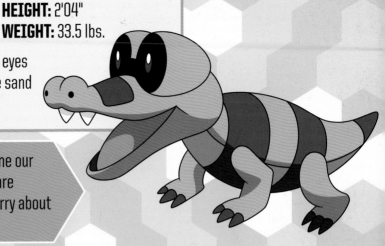

The Sandile at the spa—even the one our heroes find wearing sunglasses—are compassionate creatures that worry about the safety of others.

DEERLING (SPRING FORM)

TYPE: Normal-Grass
CATEGORY: Season Pokémon
HEIGHT: 2'00"
WEIGHT: 43.0 lbs.

With the change of each season, Deerling's appearance changes as well.

Herds of Deerling are saved by Sandile as Oshawott and Pikachu look on.

PATRAT

TYPE: Normal
CATEGORY: Scout Pokémon
HEIGHT: 1'08"
WEIGHT: 25.6 lbs.

Patrat use their tails to communicate. They keep watch over their nest in shifts and grow nervous if there's no lookout.

Patrat are saved by a bridge of Sandile near Dan's family's resort and spa.

Oshawott is ready to do battle with Ash by its side! Their first taste of a Gym battle comes in Striaton City!

STRIATON CITY

This is the first real town where Ash is able to test out his battle skills...and Oshawott! It's home to the Striaton City Gym. Rumor has it the Gym is not your normal Pokémon Gym.

Striaton City is filled with beautiful buildings, a bustling market, and very nice people. One of the first people Ash meets is Cilan, who agrees to take Ash and Iris to the Striaton Gym. But first...they stop to eat?

To the first Gym battle!

Striaton City Gym

Well, not exactly. It appears that the restaurant in Striaton City *is* the Gym, complete with a trio of battling brothers and female customers who double as cheerleaders.

Chili

Chili is sharp, and he uses the hottest material when cooking! His Pokémon is Pansear, a Fire-type Pokémon. *Sear* is another word for cooking under high heat!

PANSEAR

TYPE: Fire
CATEGORY: High Temp Pokémon
HEIGHT: 2'00"
WEIGHT: 24.3 lbs.

Pansear lives in caves near volcanoes. When Pansear is angry, the temperature on the tuft of its head can reach 600°!

Cress

Cress is after smooth taste and palatable matchups, so he uses a more fluid Pokémon, the Water-type Panpour. When measuring out the pain, this Pokémon knows how to "pour" it on.

PANPOUR

TYPE: Water
CATEGORY: Spray Pokémon
HEIGHT: 2'00"
WEIGHT: 29.8 lbs.

Panpour lived in forests long ago but developed a body that makes it easy to live near water. It can store water in the tufts on its head.

STRIATON GYM BATTLE!

A quick look at the first Gym battle
fought by Ash's Oshawott!

CILAN'S PANSAGE

VS.

ASH'S OSHAWOTT

After losing a round in the battle for the Trio Badge at the Striaton City Gym, Ash calls in Oshawott to take on Pansage. Oshawott is intimidated, but after a pep talk from Ash, it goes head-on and attacks with Tackle. Pansage easily dodges the move and counters with Bullet Seed. A couple of taunts from Cilan later, and Oshawott gets hit with Pansage's Bite.

SolarBeam

SolarBeam is a devastating move, and it's even more devastating against Water-type Pokémon!

The battle between Oshawott and Pansage is a long, drawn-out fight, but in the end, Oshawott wins with some clever moves.

It's a shock when Oshawott uses its scalchop to deflect Pansage's SolarBeam!

And when Oshawott recaptures its scalchop by bouncing Water Gun off the Gym wall, the battle is almost won.

"You'll see my awesome Oshawott's a cut above the rest!"

The Trio Badge!

After defeating Chili, Cress, and Cilan, Ash wins the Trio Badge, his first major accomplishment since arriving in Unova.

OSHAWOTT'S NEW FRIENDS

Now that Oshawott has joined Ash, here are some of its new friends!

PIDOVE

TYPE: Normal-Flying
CATEGORY: Small Pigeon Pokémon
HEIGHT: 1'00"
WEIGHT: 4.6 lbs.

A Pidove flock's cooing can get extremely noisy. Pidove is *not* attracted to shiny objects.

Ash had a Pidove in his arsenal when he challenged the Striaton City Gym, which would have made a better opponent against Pansage. But Ash had higher hopes for Oshawott!

EMOLGA

TYPE: Electric-Flying
CATEGORY: Sky Squirrel Pokémon
HEIGHT: 1'04"
WEIGHT: 11.0 lbs.

This tree-dwelling Pokémon can glide by using its cape-like membrane and discharging electricity stored inside its cheeks.

Emolga and Oshawott have a strange relationship. Oshawott is very fond of Emolga, and it is quick to defend its newfound friend. But Emolga doesn't feel the same affection for Oshawott!

PIKACHU

TYPE: Electric
CATEGORY: Mouse Pokémon
HEIGHT: 1'04"
WEIGHT: 32.2 lbs.

Pikachu's tail is sometimes struck by lightning as it raises it to check its surroundings.

Oshawott and Pikachu get along well...unless Oshawott wants the spotlight all to itself.

NEW ADVENTURES

While traveling with Oshawott, Ash and his friends visit the eerie Dreamyard. Although Oshawott didn't battle in the Dreamyard, it is surely affected by what it sees there!

The Dreamyard is an abandoned Pokémon energy research facility whose sole purpose was to explore the benefits of Musharna's Dream Mist. The scientists were supposed to find a way to make clean energy out of the mist, but the facility was destroyed when Musharna was overwhelmed by the evil and greed of people trying to use the energy for their own benefit.

There's no telling what Ash will encounter next. But with his Pokémon by his side, he knows he's up to any challenge!

SECRET MESSAGE!

Complete the words below. Take the letter
you added and rearrange them to finis
a secret message about Oshawot

A_h   Xtrans_eiver   Meowt_

Emo_ga   Dew_tt   _ansear

Stri_ton City   _ress

Oshawott loves its _ _ _ _ _ _ _ _!